FLASH
FLOOD

FLASH FLOOD

GABRIELLE PRENDERGAST

ORCA BOOK PUBLISHERS

Published in Canada and the United States
in 2024 by Orca Book Publishers.
orcabook.com

Library and Archives Canada Cataloguing in Publication
Title: Flash flood / Gabrielle Prendergast.
Names: Prendergast, Gabrielle, author.
Series: Orca anchor.
Description: Series statement: Orca anchor
Identifiers: Canadiana (print) 20230558488 | Canadiana (ebook) 20230558496 |
ISBN 9781459838215 (softcover) | ISBN 9781459840270 (PDF) |
ISBN 9781459840287 (EPUB)
Subjects: LCGFT: novels.
Classification: LCC PS8631.R448 F53 2024 | DDC jC813/.6—dc23

Library of Congress Control Number: 2023948091

Summary: In this high-interest accessible novel for teen readers,
foster brothers Zack and Peter pull together to survive after a flash flood
leaves them stranded in an evacuated neighborhood of their riverside town.

Orca Book Publishers is committed to reducing the consumption of
nonrenewable resources in the production of our books. We make
every effort to use materials that support a sustainable future.

Orca Book Publishers gratefully acknowledges the support
for its publishing programs provided by the following agencies:
the Government of Canada, the Canada Council for the Arts and
the Province of British Columbia through the BC Arts Council
and the Book Publishing Tax Credit.

Design by Ella Collier.
Cover photography by Rowan Jordan/Getty Images.
Author photo by Erika Forest.

Printed and bound in Canada.

27 26 25 24 • 1 2 3 4

Chapter One

Saturday mornings used to be quiet. That was before Peter arrived. I had three years of these quiet mornings. That's more than a lot of people can say, I guess.

Peter has been here for three months. I've been here for three years. I'm seventeen and Peter is nearly fifteen. So the same age as I was when I arrived.

Arrived in foster care. We live in a foster home with the Tates—Susan Tate and her husband, Jon Tate. They're good people.

They were so kind to me when I arrived. I had just lost my parents in a car crash. And my grandfather didn't want me. So, of course, I was a mess. Angry and sad. My thoughts all muddled. But Susan and Jon didn't expect a miracle. They gave me time.

And it took time.

For a year I acted out. I messed up at school. I got into fights. I even yelled at them. That's what I feel the worst about. I've told them I'm sorry. A bunch of times. Susan gives me a cookie each time. My mom used to say, "Cookies fix everything." Maybe all moms say that. Even foster moms.

"You were a kid with a broken heart," Susan said once when I tried to apologize. That time I took my cookie to my room. I ate it with tears streaming down my face. I still have a broken heart. But I've learned to live with it. That's what growing up is.

It isn't easy being in foster care. I have to remember that. Especially now that Saturday mornings aren't peaceful anymore.

Now Peter is the one acting out. He has been skipping school. So the Tates took his phone away. He's yelling at them in the kitchen. Jon is trying to calm Peter down, but it's not working. I'm in my room, trying to do my homework.

"You're not my dad!" Peter says.

Oh boy. I've said that a few times. It's different when Peter says it. My dad is dead. Peter's dad is alive. He's just not a good dad. He hits Peter's mom. And they both got arrested for drugs. It's very messy.

Peter tells me all kinds of stuff. Sometimes when he starts talking, he can't stop. It's the ADHD. I have it too. I take medicine for it, but I'm not sure if I always will. The doctor says it will help me at school. But outside of school, I might not need it. It depends on what job I do.

I'd like to work outdoors. With nature or animals. I make pocket money mowing lawns in town. Or weeding gardens. When I'm outdoors, my brain doesn't feel so buzzy.

I think Peter's brain buzzes no matter where he is.

"I hate you!" Peter yells. "I hate both of you! I hate Zack too!"

That's me. Zack. I don't think Peter really hates me. But it still hurts to hear it.

The door slams. I look out the window. Peter stomps across the lawn. He must be really mad. It's pouring rain, and the road is covered in puddles. Water soaks his shoes. He turns down our street. I watch him until he disappears around the corner.

He'll come back. I always came back. And he'll get better, grow up a bit. Just like I did.

I wasn't sure about Peter moving in. The Tates asked me. They didn't need to do that.

We sat down and talked about it. At first I wanted to say no. But then I remembered how much the Tates had helped me. I didn't want to be selfish. I remembered what Susan had said about my broken heart. Did Peter have a broken heart too? What if he somehow found out I didn't want him? That would make it even worse. So I said yes.

Jon said he was proud of me. That felt good. Then he said I would be like a big brother to Peter. That felt weird. Susan just smiled and gave me a cookie.

I've grown two pant sizes since I moved in here.

I sigh and look out the window again. Maybe Peter will be smart and come back soon. The rain pours down. I watch the road.

I listen to Jon and Susan talking in low voices in the kitchen. I can't hear what they're saying. I can imagine, though. They're talking about Peter. Everything is about Peter now.

I know it's wrong to be jealous. I'm older. I can take care of myself. I don't mess up anymore. So why should they talk about me? It's dumb. Messed-up kids get attention. Good kids get left alone. That seems unfair. But that's the way it is.

Maybe I should just ask for a cookie.

At least the house will be quiet for a while.

Chapter Two

Peter has told me a lot about his family. His real family. He told me once he woke up in the morning and his mom and dad were gone. There were a bunch of people in his house. They were all wasted on drugs. But none of them were his parents. He was only five or six. A lady gave him cold pizza. He drank water from the bath tap. He couldn't find a cup.

Then the police came. His mom was in hospital. His dad came home. Promised the police he'd smarten up. But he didn't.

When I try to imagine the scene, Peter looks like a little elf. He's still not very big. He has light-blond hair, wide-set blue eyes and a tiny nose. He says he didn't cry. Even when they told him about his mom.

I don't like to think about his family. I know they're terrible. But at least they're alive. And his mom wanted to keep him. Maybe his dad did too. But they weren't allowed. They'd had chance after chance. They kept screwing it up. They'd get high and leave Peter alone. His dad would get violent. His mom would drive drunk. Peter wasn't safe with them.

But he can talk to them on the phone. He doesn't do it often. But he can.

When I want to talk to my parents, I have to go to the graveyard. And I don't think they hear me. At least, they never answer.

And my grandfather. My mom's dad. The only other family I have. He didn't need any chances to keep me. He just didn't want to. Susan says I can call him. Or write to him if I feel like it. But I don't.

Peter told me he doesn't have grandparents.

Some of the kids in my school have all four of them. And they see them all the time. One girl in my class has six grandparents. Her mother's parents got divorced and both remarried. She's also got over twenty cousins.

It's not fair. Some people have such big families. While I have no one.

Except the Tates.

"Zack, honey?" Susan calls out from the kitchen. "Come eat supper!"

Her happy voice cheers me up. Nothing seems to bother her. It's dark outside. It's raining. And Peter still hasn't come back. But Susan is calling me to eat supper. Just like nothing is wrong.

Maybe supper is a bit quieter than usual. Part of that is because Peter is not here. But Susan and Jon are quiet too. Susan keeps looking at the side door. Jon keeps glancing at his watch. The rain makes a fuzzy static noise. Like when Jon can't find the right radio station in the car. I like that noise.

I know people complain about the rain. Lately there's even been a lot of talk about floods. People are scared it's raining too much. It's from climate change, they say. I see it on the news. Villages getting washed away. People losing their homes.

But I like the rain. It makes me feel peaceful.

"Do you have any idea where Peter would go?" Jon asks me suddenly. The peaceful rainy feeling goes away.

I shrug. "He's not from around here," I say. "And I don't know who his friends are."

"What about at school?" Susan asks. "Has he made new friends there?"

I look down at my plate. Chicken curry and rice. One of my favorites. But I'm losing my appetite.

"I don't really see him at school," I say. He's in ninth grade, and I'm in eleventh. And maybe I should check up on him in school. I am supposed to be his brother, after all. But I have my own friends. And I can't be everywhere all the time. "He eats lunch in the film room."

Lots of kids do. The weird kids mostly. Our film teacher shows movies at lunchtime. I used to eat in there. But I'm more popular now.

I take a sip of my water. I wish we could talk about something else. I wish Peter would just come back.

"We have to give Peter a little more time," Susan says.

"I know," I say. "He'll settle in. Just like I did."

Jon nods. He and Susan look at each other.

"It's just that...things might be a little harder for him," Susan says.

"You mean because of his FASD?" I ask. Then I press my lips together. I look down at my plate again. I wasn't supposed to know about that. FASD is fetal alcohol spectrum disorder. Kids can get it if their mother drinks alcohol while she's pregnant.

"We...didn't know you knew about that," Jon says carefully.

"Peter told me," I say. The first night he was here, in fact.

Susan nods. "And you know what it means?" she asks.

I repeat all the things Peter told me. He said the FASD makes him slow to learn. And clumsy. And sometimes he makes bad choices.

Like running out into the rain and not coming back.

Jon and Susan watch me. They look pretty serious.

"It's not…like, it's not going to kill him or anything, is it?" I ask. Peter didn't mention anything about it being fatal. But maybe he doesn't know.

Susan reaches out and squeezes my hand. "No. No. Nothing like that."

"But things will always be a bit harder for him," Jon says. "Probably."

"What about medication?" I ask. "Like what I take for ADHD?"

"We thought that might help," Jon says. "But it doesn't seem to."

"Maybe something else will," I say. It's the kind of thing Susan would say. She thinks there's help for everyone somewhere.

"Maybe," Susan says. "But we just want you to understand. We need to spend some time on Peter. We don't want you to think...well...you know."

That they're ignoring me. That they're favoring Peter. All things I did think a bit. Even though I knew why, I still didn't like it. I start feeling very mixed-up inside. But I don't want to show that.

"It's okay," I say. "I totally understand. Anyway, I'm not a little kid anymore."

Outside the wind gusts. The trees smack against the window.

"I'm going to go out and look for him," Jon says. "He can't stay out all night in this."

"Why don't you both go?" I say it without thinking. But it does make sense. "You both have cars. One can look east and one west. Or something. I'll wait here. I can call you if he comes back."

Susan stands and starts clearing the dishes. "That's probably a good idea," she says. "He could be anywhere. And it's cold."

I jump to my feet and take the plates from her. "I'll clean up the kitchen," I say. It's like a fully grown adult has come to life inside me. "I'll take care of everything here. You go look for him. We're in this together."

Susan hugs me around the dishes in my hands.

Jon musses my hair. "We love you, kid," he says.

I hold it together until they are out the door. I watch them get into their cars. Then I let a few tears drip into the sink.

Like I said. Broken heart.

Chapter Three

I clean the whole kitchen. Run the dishwasher. Mop the floor. Wipe out the sink. When the dishwasher is done, I put everything away. Then I reorganize the fridge. Then the cupboards. I'm scrolling through recipes for butter tarts when I finally take a breath. I look at the time on my phone.

It's after ten. I've been buzzing around in the kitchen for hours. I get like that in the evenings sometimes. It's because I take a pill for ADHD in the morning. It wears off. I get tired like a normal kid. But then I start bouncing off the walls. Susan and Jon are usually here to tell me to get into bed.

I'm kind of hungry, though. I make myself a bowl of cereal. I watch the rain pour down while I eat it. Then I wash out the bowl and spoon. I dry them and put them away. Leaving the kitchen light on, I go to my room.

For some reason I just get into bed in my clothes. It's like I suddenly realize how tired I am. As soon as I close my eyes, I'm asleep.

I wake up to my phone blaring at me. Groggy, I grab for it. There's a message on the screen.

EMERGENCY ALERT: MANDATORY EVACUATION.

What the heck?

I sit up and try to turn on my lamp. Nothing happens.

"The power is out?" I say to the dark.

Then someone starts banging on the front door. Peter!

I jump out of bed. In the dark I slam my toes into the side of my dresser. I bite back a swear.

Feeling my way down the hall, I reach the front door and yank it open.

"You are in so much troub—"

But it's not Peter. It's Mr. and Mrs. Lee. Our neighbors.

"Did you get the alert?" Mrs. Lee says. She's wearing a bright-yellow raincoat and high rubber boots.

"Yes!" I say. "It woke me up. Susan and Jon aren't here."

"I know," Mrs. Lee says. "Susan called us. They're still looking for Peter."

Mr. Lee splashes back to their car. It's parked on the street at the end of their driveway. When he opens the door, the interior light comes on. I can see the Lees' three little kids in the back seat. They stare out at me. Both their dogs press their noses against the car window too. The window is streaming with rain.

Their headlights shine up the road.

"We're evacuating," Mrs. Lee says. "The levee broke."

I shake my head. Maybe this is a dream. I saw a video about the levee breaking in New Orleans. It was terrible. A bunch of people died. Thousands lost their homes. Is that going to happen here?

"We have room for you in the car," Mrs. Lee says. "Susan is stuck on the other side of Abbotsford. Jon is in Chilliwack. We can take you up to the school. It's on higher ground. People are sleeping there."

We live about a ten-minute drive south

of Abbotsford. There are some little rows of houses tucked in between farms. But it's flat and low. Just the right kind of land for a flood.

"What about Peter?" I realize we're yelling. The wind and rain are so loud. This feels like a movie scene.

Just then my phone vibrates in my hand. Jon is calling!

"Hello?"

"Have you left?" he yells. "With the Lees?"

"Did you find Peter?"

"Don't worry about that," Jon says. "You need to get out. Grab your stuff and go with the Lees. I think the highway might get closed. If it does I won't be able to get back."

"We need to hurry!" Mrs. Lee says.

I nod and go back into the house. I turn on my phone's flashlight and put Jon on speaker. Grabbing my backpack, I head toward the kitchen. Yes, I'm thinking about snacks—I'm a teenager. I'm hungry all the time. But as soon as I get into the kitchen, the side door opens.

Peter is standing there. Soaking wet and blue with cold.

"Jon!" I say into the phone. "Peter just walked in!"

"Thank God!" Jon says. And he sounds very relieved. "I'm on the highway now. I think I can make it back. I don't think the Lees have room for two more. They said they'd have to squeeze you in."

I pull Peter inside and shove him into a kitchen chair. His teeth are chattering.

Back at the front door I talk to Mrs. Lee. "You don't have room for both of us, right?"

She looks apologetic. "I'm sorry. No. With the kids and the dogs and the supplies, we barely fit."

"I can make it back," Jon says over the phone. My head is starting to spin. I hate trying to talk to two people at once.

"You go," I say to Mrs. Lee. "Jon is on his way back."

Mrs. Lee hesitates.

"We'll be fine," I say. Then I watch her splash back to her car. They drive off through deep puddles.

"I'm thirty minutes away," Jon says. We sign off.

"You!" I say to Peter when I get back into the kitchen. "Go put on some dry clothes."

Digging in the kitchen drawer, I find a flashlight. Peter takes it down the hall to his room. He doesn't say anything. I'm glad for that. If he starts making excuses, I'm going to lose it.

I light a candle. And I manage to get the gas stove lit. I heat up some of tonight's curry and boil some water for tea. While I wait, I pack some food into the backpack.

Peter comes back to the kitchen. He's in dry clothes. When he sits down and starts eating, I bring the candle over and put it on the table. We shouldn't waste the flashlight batteries. I sit across from him.

"Where did you go?" I ask finally.

Peter slurps his tea. He's stopped shivering. His damp hair is sticking up all over his head.

"Nowhere," he says. "I just walked around."

"For more than twelve hours?"

"I took a nap at the library," he says. "But they kicked me out at six."

I should have thought of that. I used to go to the library sometimes. When I needed to be alone. To cool off on hot days. To have some time to think.

"Jon and Susan have been really worried," I say.

The candlelight makes Peter's face look hollow. He has dark circles under his eyes.

I wish tonight was a normal night. I could try to really talk to him. Or Susan could make cookies. I know Peter is not doing well. But I don't know what to do. Or if anything I do will even help.

I take his empty bowl and cup and rinse them out in the sink.

"We need to pack a few things," I say. "We've got to evacuate."

Chapter Four

I find another flashlight in the hall closet.
Peter takes it to his room to pack. I check the
food I've already packed. Then I add more.
I check the closet for anything waterproof.
I have a pretty good raincoat. I try on a pair
of Susan's rain boots. They're too small. But
I leave them out. They might fit Peter.

"Make sure you put on another sweater!" I yell down to his room.

Peter has the small room at the end of the hall. It used to be Susan's office when she was teaching online. But now she teaches at the college. Jon works at the border crossing. They moved their schedules around so one of them can always be home after school. That was for Peter. He needs a bit more supervision than I do. But he's been skipping school a lot. So who knows what he's been doing.

Sometimes I want to shake him. Does he even know how much the Tates do for him? I wish I could explain how good they've been to me.

"And pack extra socks!" I yell. Peter doesn't answer. "Peter?"

I go to his room. The door is closed. Maybe he's changing again. I knock lightly, but he doesn't answer. Has he gone to sleep? I don't blame him. He must be exhausted. But we need to get going.

Shining the flashlight in, I nudge the door open.

Peter is sitting on the floor, the screen of his phone lighting up his face. He has earbuds in.

"Hey!" I yell.

He twitches and pulls out his earbuds.

"What are you doing?" I ask him. "Where did you find your phone?"

"It was in Susan's dresser," he answers. "Where it always is."

I step forward and grab it out of his hands. He doesn't protest as I shove the phone into my pocket. "You're not supposed to have this," I say. "And you're not supposed to go through Susan's things. What is wrong with you?"

"What is wrong with *you*?" he snarls back.

"I'm annoyed," I say. "There's a natural disaster going on. And you're acting like an ungrateful child. You *are* an ungrateful child. Have you even packed anything?"

Peter stands, making a frustrated noise. "Fine. I'll pack!" he says. He yanks one of his drawers right out of his dresser. Then he throws the whole thing against the wall. It smashes into pieces.

I take a step back. Peter is a little wild, but I've never seen him like this. He seems to realize what he's done. Diving across his bed, he picks up the broken drawer. His clothes spill everywhere as he tries to put the pieces of wood back together.

"I'll fix it. I'm sorry. I'm sorry!" he says, frantic.

I move toward him, and he tumbles off the bed. Crouching down, he pulls his blanket over his head.

"Sorry sorry sorry," he says.

I step around the bed. Peter pokes his head out of the blanket.

I don't know what's going on. I think Peter is scared. I think his real parents hit him sometimes. Susan and Jon never told me that exactly. But I suspected it.

"It's okay," I say. "I'm not...I'm mad about the drawer. You shouldn't have broken it. But I'm not going to hit you. I would never do that. Neither would Susan or Jon. You're safe here."

He lets the blanket fall down. Curled up like that on the floor, he looks even smaller than usual. I wish I had time to have a good talk with him. But we need to get ready to leave. I can't just pretend nothing is wrong, though.

"I'll help you pack," I say. "Where's your backpack?"

"Someone stole it," Peter says. "I got jumped in the park."

"What?! Are you okay?"

Peter pulls himself up to sit on the bed. "Yeah," he says. "They just grabbed my backpack and ran off."

"What was in your backpack?" I ask.

He shrugs. "A few clothes. My toothbrush. My pills and stuff."

"Your pills?" I think about that for a second. "You were running away?"

Peter shrugs again.

"Why?" I ask. "Where did you think you might go?"

"Home, I guess," he says.

I sit on the bed next to him. I'm not sure what to say. I don't know if the Tates want

Peter to know how much they've told me about him. But I can't have him running off again. Running off toward something that doesn't exist.

The flashlight shines on the ceiling. Peter waves his fingers in front of it. He makes a crocodile mouth with the shadow.

"You can't go home," I finally say. "Your parents don't live there anymore. Your dad went to Victoria. He's homeless. And your mom moved back to Ontario. You know this, don't you?"

Peter sighs and lies back on the bed. I shine the flashlight down on him.

"Did you take your pills today at least? Before they got stolen?"

"No."

I have to try really hard not to show how frustrated I am. I close my eyes for a second and think.

"Find a shopping bag by the side door," I say. "Put some clean clothes in there. Warm clothes. There are new toothbrushes under the sink in the bathroom. Take one of those. I'm going to call Jon."

I leave him and go back to the kitchen. I check my own backpack, zipping it up.

Then I take out my phone. My battery is at 10 percent, and I have no way to charge it. I swear under my breath. Then I call Jon's number.

All I hear is a weird beep. Then a voice says, "Your call cannot be completed." I try again, but I get the same message. I decide to send a text instead.

Peter says he didn't take his medication today. But it got stolen with his backpack. What should I do?

I send the same message to Susan.

Then I wait, listening to the sound of Peter digging around in his closet.

But Susan and Jon don't reply.

Chapter Five

Ten minutes later Peter says he's packed. He lets me check his bag. He has packed underwear and socks. A pair of jeans and two T-shirts. He's wearing a hoodie over a sweater. I put some granola bars in his bag. And the rest of the apples. We finish the milk from the fridge. He tries on

Susan's rain boots. They fit. We both put on raincoats.

The power is still off. My phone is at 8 percent. Peter's phone is at 5 percent. And neither Susan nor Jon has texted back. It's been over an hour since Peter turned up. Jon and I spoke right after that, when he said he was thirty minutes away. I don't know what to do but wait.

Peter and I sit across the kitchen table. The candle is still burning. Wax drips down. There are a few other candles in the drawer. I pack two of them and some matches.

"What medications were in your back-pack?" I ask Peter. "What got stolen?"

Peter lists his ADHD pills—the same ones I take—and some other stuff.

"For my asthma," Peter says. "But I'll be okay. I don't have...I haven't...it's been a while... you know...I don't need..."

I interrupt him. "Good, okay." I remember when it was hard for me to finish a sentence. "We can worry about that later."

Peter's knees bounce under the table. People think ADHD is just having a lot of energy. Like it might be fun. But it's not fun most of the time. It's like having someone poking you. Or five people talking to you at once. You bounce and fidget. Your muscles feel weird. And it's like there's a storm in your brain a lot of the time.

It's true that sometimes we can get really focused on something. Peter draws hundreds of pictures of cars. Pretty good pictures. I'll weed and tidy a garden for hours. It will look perfect when I'm done. But when you're a kid in school, there's other stuff you're supposed to do. Remember your homework. Study for tests. Concentrate. Stay quiet in class. All of that is hard with ADHD.

The wind makes the windows rattle. Peter jiggles in his chair. Weirdly, I feel pretty calm. Maybe this storm is like gardening for me. It's helping keep my brain focused.

"Were you in other foster homes before this?" I ask. I'll get him talking a bit. Maybe he'll relax.

"Oh yeah. Tons," Peter says. "I got put with foster parents when I was still a baby. But then my real parents got me back. Then it happened again. And again."

"That must have been hard," I say.

"Yeah. One time I was…when I…a foster mom…I was about ten…and I…a foster mom bought me a suitcase," Peter says. "Then because…it was…I got…got…got…moved to another foster home. So I took it…took the suitcase with me. But then one of the other kids there…in that home…the other…they got moved. And they took my suitcase! So I was… I told my case worker and she said…"

He rambles and gets distracted as he goes on. But eventually he finishes the story. His case worker drove him around to five different foster homes. Trying to find the suitcase. Finally they figured out someone took it to France. They never brought it back.

"And now my backpack is gone too," Peter says. "I have bad luck with luggage."

I don't mean to laugh. But that was funny. And I have a weird giggle, so that makes Peter laugh. We sit there in the candlelight, giggling.

Suddenly Peter puts his hand up. "Shhh," he says. "Did you hear that?"

All I can hear is the rain.

"Hear what?"

Peter goes over to the side door. He opens it. Cold air rushes in.

"Hey..." I start. But then I hear it too. A dog barking.

"Is that Misty or Pompom?" Peter asks. Misty and Pompom are Mrs. Lee's dogs. They're both miniature poodles. Their barks are high-pitched. Annoying, if I'm being honest.

I hear it again. Definitely not high-pitched. A low *woof, woof, woof.* It sounds like a big dog.

Peter flicks on his flashlight and shines it outside. "Holy…wow," he says.

"What?" I jump up and join him at the door.

Oh.

Oh no.

The street is flooded! Our yard is mostly under water!

The dog barks again.

"It's coming from out back!" Peter says. He yells to be heard over the rain. "Come on!"

We're already in our rain gear. So we slosh out into the driveway. Turning, we head down behind the house. It backs onto farmland. I don't know the farmers that well. Their house is actually pretty far away. But I hope they got out.

"It's in the field!" Peter says. He shines his flashlight out. The farmland is under water too. But sure enough, there's a dog there. It's perched on top of a giant hay bale. Barking its head off.

Before I can stop him, Peter climbs over the fence. He sloshes into the field. The water is up past his knees. So much for changing into dry clothes. I have to follow him.

We can barely see where we're stepping. I hold my flashlight over my head. And hope it's waterproof. But a few very wet minutes later, we reach the dog.

It looks like a Labrador retriever. It's wearing a collar. So it's probably not a stray.

"Poor puppy!" Peter says. "Did you get left behind?"

The dog woofs. It picks its way down off the hay bale. I hand Peter my flashlight and hold my arms out. The dog climbs right into them.

"Oof. You're heavy!" I say.

Peter shines the flashlight back toward the house. I follow him. My boots squelch in the mud. I hope I don't get stuck. The dog just licks my face.

"Okay," I say. "I've got you."

Peter clambers back over the fence. As I hoist the dog over, I see its collar. There's a name on it. "Annie." I guess she's a girl.

Annie drops into water up to her neck. She barks as I climb over the fence. I lift her up and carry her back to the house.

Water runs down the driveway like a river. When we get to the side door, my heart sinks.

Peter opens the door, and we see. The house is flooded. A good six inches of water covers the kitchen floor.

And it's still rising.

Chapter Six

"What do we do?" Peter asks. He sounds scared. I'm scared too. But someone needs to be the brave one. I have to think.

Last year I watched a show about Hurricane Katrina. When the water rose there, people went up to their attics. But then they got trapped. A bunch of people died that way.

I think about the street we're on. It's a gentle downhill slope. I used to practice my skateboarding on it. I'd walk up to the corner near the main road. Then I'd ride back down to our house.

Our house. My house. That's weird. I used to think of it as Susan and Jon's house. I'm not sure when that changed. Maybe just in time for it to be destroyed by a flood.

But the main road is on higher ground. It might not be underwater. And it's not far away. In fact, maybe Jon is up there. Maybe he can't get through the flood with his car. We're already soaking wet anyway.

Annie barks as though she agrees with what I'm thinking. She's the reason we're soaking wet.

"I think we should head out on foot," I say.

Peter just looks back at me, face grim.

Before we go, I find Susan's box of photos. It has photos of her parents. Of Jon's parents. She showed them all to me just after I moved in. They're old photos. The kind taken with an old camera. Which means there are no digital versions.

I pull down the attic stairs. Then I carry the box of photos up there. Peter brings up Jon's and Susan's laptops and the one Peter and I share. And the video game console. And his sketchbooks.

By the time we're done, the water is a foot deep in the hallway. But maybe it won't get much higher. Maybe the stuff in the attic will be safe. Maybe we'd be safe up there too. But I don't want to risk it.

We find Annie perched on the kitchen table. I tie a length of rope to her collar. When I give it a tug, she jumps down. The water is up to her chest. She doesn't seem too bothered by it.

Just before I lock the doors, I remember Jon's safety briefing. Another thing that happened just after I arrived. Jon took me around the house and showed me all the safety stuff. Where the fire extinguishers are. A laminated list of emergency numbers. I shove the list in my backpack. Then I find the electric panel. I turn the power completely off. I turn off the main water tap too. And the gas. We practice this once a year.

Jon would be proud of me.

I lock the door. Shove the keys into my coat pocket. Zip it shut. Then we slosh out into the street.

Peter holds the flashlight. He walks in front. I follow, tugging Annie along.

The water is deeper than I thought. Annie has to swim part of the way. And it takes longer than I expect to get up to the main road. By the time we reach it, Peter and I are both soaked to the waist. There's a car on the main road. Not Jon's. Not anyone's I know. And it's empty. Locked.

The water is still ankle-deep. No sign of anyone else around. Annie climbs up onto the car to get out of the wet. She barks.

Peter shines the flashlight back down our street. It looks like a lake at night. The rain is not as heavy as it was. But the damage is done. It feels like the end of the world.

I give Annie's rope leash to Peter and take the flashlight. I shine it up and down the main road. In one direction it's underwater. In the other direction, toward town, it looks like it might be clear. We slosh that way. Annie resists at first. But I take her leash from Peter and yank it, and she jumps after us.

After another few minutes we finally reach dry ground. Well, not dry exactly. But at least not underwater anymore. It's so dark. I feel like we're in space. Or some kind of nightmare land. Faintly, through the dark, I see the outline of something up the road. A house! And it's on a little hill. It's not flooded! Annie sees the house too. She tugs on her leash.

"Maybe there's someone home," I say.

Peter doesn't answer. He is shivering. So is Annie.

We head up to the house. The driveway is not under water. But it's muddy. We leave dirty tracks when we cross the porch to the front door. I knock. No one answers. I try again. Annie barks. Nothing. No one is home.

I feel like screaming. What else could go wrong today? It's like Mother Nature wants us to drown. Or freeze. It's so cold I can see my breath. And we're soaking wet. We need to get dry.

"Maybe we could break in," Peter says.

"Do you know how to break into a house?" I ask.

"Of course."

We stare at each other for a second. Then I burst out laughing. Poor Peter had a hard childhood. But I guess he learned some useful skills. Minutes later he has climbed through a window and opened the front door for us.

Annie runs in. It's like she knows the place. Or maybe she's just relieved to be inside. I shine the flashlight around. Everything is dry. We find some towels and blankets. There's even a fireplace! In moments Peter has a nice fire going. Another skill he learned as a kid maybe.

We all sit around the fire. My toes and fingers start to warm up. We each have an apple, and Annie eats the cores.

"Do you think we can sleep here?" Peter asks.

"I don't know," I say.

I watch the fire. When I turn back to Peter, he and Annie are curled up together. Asleep. I pull another blanket over them. I wrap one around myself. My eyelids start to feel very heavy. I should probably stay awake to watch over us. But maybe I'll close my eyes for a few seconds.

Just…

A few…

Seconds…

Chapter Seven

Something smacks me on the leg. I open my eyes, but it's pitch dark. I squirm. The blanket is over my head. When I pull it down, I can still barely see.

Something whacks me again.

"Ow!" I yelp.

"What are you doing in my house?" someone says.

Oh no.

I sit up, squinting in the dark. A tall shadow hangs over me. Is that a rifle poking into my leg? I raise my hands.

"Don't shoot!" I say. "We were cold. We got caught in the flood."

A flashlight clicks on, shining in my eyes. I still can't see who the shadow is. But I can see that the rifle is actually a hockey stick.

"You're the Tates' kid, aren't you?" the voice says. He moves the hockey stick away from my leg. "I'm Dev Preet." He shines the flashlight on his face. "This is my parents' place. I came back to look for their dog. Annie."

I know the Preets. Susan buys corn on the cob from their market stall every year.

Wait. Annie?

I look beside me. Peter and Annie look like a giant pile of blankets. I pull the blankets away. Peter stirs. Annie pops her head up.

"Annie!" Dev says.

Annie barks and leaps to her feet. Her tail wags. Dev tosses the hockey stick away. He bends over to give Annie a scratch.

"You broke a window," Dev says to me.

"We'll pay for it," I say. "We were a bit desperate."

"Hmm," Dev says with a frown. "At least you found our dog. She got scared and ran off when my parents were packing the car. Where was she?"

"In the field behind our house," I say. "We were trying to get up out of the flood. But this is as far as we got."

"Yeah. The road is flooded," Dev says. "The highway is out."

"Who are you?" Peter asks, rubbing his eyes.

We do some proper introductions. Dev offers to see if there's any food in the kitchen. Soon we're eating cold samosas at the dining table.

"The road up to town is not that bad," Dev says. "My truck can make it." He pours us both some milk. Even though the fridge was off, it's still pretty cold. I gulp it down. Dev continues, "When we're done eating, I'll take you up there. People are sheltering at the school. Unless you have somewhere else to go."

"We…thanks," I say. I'll figure out where to go once we get to Abbotsford. Hopefully, we can find the Tates. I try to call them on Dev's phone, but I still can't get through.

"Some of the cell towers are down," Dev says.

We clear away our mess as much as we can. Then Dev carries Annie out to his truck. Peter coughs and sniffs as we follow Dev.

The drive up the flooded road is slow. The sun is coming up. I look out the window. It's stopped raining. The sky is clearing. But all around us are farms and fields underwater. We pass the winery. The chicken farm where we get eggs. The garden center. All of it is gone. In the back seat, his face smushed against Annie, his feet tangled with Dev's hockey sticks, Peter sleeps. Maybe he's too young to understand. All these people are going to lose their homes.

We're going to lose our home.

Dev is silent as he drives. With the rising sun on his face, I can see his grim expression. He must be thinking the same thing as me.

"Did…did anyone die?" I ask quietly. I don't want to wake Peter. Even over the truck engine, I can hear him wheezing.

"We don't know yet," Dev says.

"I watched a show about Hurricane Katrina," I say.

"It won't be that bad," Dev says.

We don't make it into Abbotsford. The highway is deep underwater right where it meets the main road we're on. A bunch of cars are abandoned there. More are half-drowned in the parking lot of a drugstore.

"This is deeper than it was last night," Dev says. He wades out into the water. At the deepest point, it's up to his chest. He sloshes back. "If we get across this, we can walk," he says. "We can get up the hill at least. Find somewhere dry."

Peter looks pale when I wake him. He coughs as he climbs out of the truck. I hope he's not catching a cold. I wouldn't be surprised. It's freezing. I can barely feel my hands and feet.

Dev puts Annie on his shoulders and leads us into the water. At the deepest point, Peter is up to his neck.

"Get on my back," I say. I hoist him up and piggyback him the rest of the way.

When we reach dry land, I let him down. He collapses in a pile on the road, coughing.

"I can't…breathe…" he says.

"What?" Dev says. "What happened?"

Peter looks very pale now. He's gasping.

"It's asthma!" I say. "Do you have your inhaler?"

"I…lost…it…stolen…" Peter says.

"How far are we from the hospital?" I ask.

Dev is already on his phone, trying 9-1-1. "I can't get through," he says. "The hospital is about a twenty-minute walk."

"Too far." Peter has started to cry. "I can't breathe…" he gasps.

"Stay with him," I say.

Dev helps Peter sit up as I dive back into the deep water. I swim this time. It's freezing, but I can't think about that. Peter could die.

Another safety talk I had with Jon and Susan was what to do if Peter had an asthma attack. How to help him use his inhaler.

I get to Dev's truck. I grab a hockey stick from the back. The water in the parking lot is only knee-deep. I run, splashing everywhere.

When I reach the drugstore, I don't hesitate. I smash the glass door with the handle of the hockey stick. I expect an alarm to go off. But nothing happens.

The asthma inhalers aren't hard to find. There's a whole shelf of them in the pharmacy section. I grab a handful, shoving them in a plastic bag. I hold the bag over my head as I slosh back to Peter and Dev.

Dev tears at the cardboard wrapper on one of the inhalers. Peter tries to take it, but his hands are trembling and weak. Annie barks as I help him. I shake the inhaler and shove it into his mouth. He exhales as much as he can. I press the inhaler. Peter inhales as it hisses out the medication.

We do it three more times.

Finally, after what feels like forever, Peter takes a proper breath.

Chapter Eight

Dev and I let Peter lie on the road for a few minutes. Annie licks his face. But we need to keep moving. Apart from anything else, we're soaking wet. And it's cold.

"We should head toward the hospital," Dev says.

"Yeah, or..." I look at the nearby hills because I've just realized where we are. There's a house up there I know. I don't want to go there. But maybe I have to.

"Come this way," I say.

We turn off the highway and onto a side road. It leads to some houses on the hill. The roads are dry here. Annie follows us happily. Once we reach the houses, I even see a porch light on.

"They have power!" I say.

"Where...are we...going?" Peter asks. He's still wheezing a bit. Dev lets him climb on for another piggyback. I take a proper look at Dev. He's older than us. Probably in his twenties. And pretty big. He's carrying Peter like it's nothing.

"You're strong," I say.

"I play for the Chiefs," he says.

"The Chilliwack Chiefs?" That's one of the local hockey teams. I've seen them play. "That explains the hockey sticks."

"Yep," Dev says, grinning. "Where *are* we going?"

I walk for a moment before answering. "My grandpa's house."

The house I should be living in. I love Susan and Jon, and they love me. But family is family. Blood is blood. My grandfather should have stepped up. And he didn't. He took me in the night Mom and Dad died. The days after that are a blur. Police. Funeral. And meetings with social workers. Then, before I knew it, I was in foster care. Three years later and I'm still mad about it. But his house is at the end of this street. And I'm desperate.

To get Peter warm. To dry off. To find Jon and Susan.

After another few minutes, we reach it. Grandpa's house.

It looks just like I remember. A small bungalow with faded green paint. Overgrown garden. A sign reading *No Junk Mail* by the mailbox.

I take a breath as I walk up to the door. Then I hold that breath as I knock.

It takes a long time for anything to happen. I'm about to suggest we leave when the door opens.

Grandpa is standing there. "Zack!" he says.

Why am I surprised that he recognizes me? I haven't changed that much.

"Thank God!" He steps back, ushering me in. "Get in here. Susan and Jon have been worried sick!"

I point back to Dev and Peter. "My friends…"

"Yes, yes. All of you, get in here. Dog too."

Grandpa wanders away from the door. I notice he walks with a cane. Did he always have a cane? As Dev and Peter come in and close the door, Grandpa makes a call on his ancient landline.

"Yes, he just came to my door," he says into the phone. He looks me over. "He's soaking wet. So are the other boys…I don't know. There's another boy. And a dog. Who are you?" Grandpa says to Dev.

"Dev Preet. The Tates know my parents. This is Annie."

"Did you hear that?" Grandpa says. "Okay. Bye." He hangs up.

I kind of wanted to talk to Susan and Jon. Oh well.

Grandpa shuffles over to a chair and eases into it. He fiddles with some plastic tubing, fitting it into his nose.

"Let me help you with that, sir," Dev says.

"Is that oxygen?" I ask. I look around. There's an oxygen tank next to the chair. One of those walker things by the door. A bunch of pill bottles on the kitchen table.

"Are you sick, Grandpa?" I ask.

"Just the COPD," he says. "Like always."

"I have asthma," Peter says. He almost sounds proud.

"My lungs are trash," Grandpa says. "Have been for years. You knew that."

"Is that—" I start. But then I don't finish. Because I know the answer. Yes, that is the reason Grandpa didn't take me when Mom and Dad died. Of course it is. I knew that. But I didn't see it that way until right this minute. Grandpa is way too sick to take care of me.

Suddenly I'm thinking of those first days and weeks. And months. How angry I was. How I wouldn't listen to anyone. Or talk to anyone. Is this what they'd been trying to tell me? That Grandpa would have taken me if he weren't so sick?

Every time Susan had suggested I call Grandpa, I'd said no. Because I thought he had rejected me.

He must have been grieving too. His daughter and son-in-law were dead.

He'd sent me birthday and Christmas cards. I'd spent the twenty dollars inside on junk food. But thrown away the cards without even reading them. I look around the tiny, old house and realize that Grandpa probably struggled to afford that twenty dollars.

What is wrong with me? My face burns with shame.

"It's good to see you, my boy," Grandpa says. "You've certainly grown. Dev and Peter, why don't you dig around in my closet for some towels and dry clothes? Then I think I can manage to make some tea and toast if you'll help me, Zack."

Annie follows Dev and Peter into the bedroom. I hoist Grandpa out of his chair and help him to the little kitchen. The oxygen tank wheels along with him. In seconds the kettle is boiling. And Grandpa is sitting again, this time at the table.

Dev comes back with a tracksuit for me. I duck into the bathroom and change. I towel my hair and look at my face in the mirror. I feel like an idiot. And the worst grandson who ever lived.

But I did save Peter's life today. And last night I rescued a dog.

When I get back to the kitchen, Dev, Annie and Peter are gone.

"The little one started wheezing again," Grandpa says. "The big one took my car to run him up to the hospital. Your foster parents will meet them there. Then they'll come back here for you. Okay to hang with your grandpa for a while?"

"Okay," I say. There are cookies on the table. Grandpa pours me some nice hot tea.

"Sit down and tell me everything," he says.

I sit down. I don't even know where to start. So I go with something familiar.

"I'm sorry," I say. "For being mad at you. For not wanting to talk to you. I guess I didn't understand. But I understand now."

Grandpa just shakes his head. "Have a cookie," he says.

READ ON FOR AN EXCERPT FROM
AFTERSHOCK

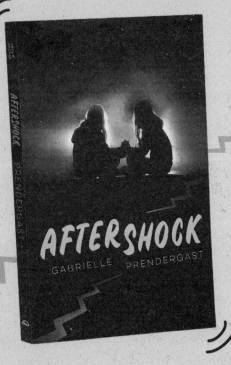

AFTERSHOCK

GABRIELLE PRENDERGAST

WHAT WILL BE LEFT WHEN THE WORLD STOPS SHAKING?

After a massive earthquake hits, Amy finds herself alone with Mara, a half sister she hardly knows. Together they set out on a perilous journey from their suburb into the city to search for their parents.

Chapter One

Finally! It's the last day of school. I'm happy. Summer is going to be great. I made some new friends this year, and we're going to hang out. Go on hikes. Maybe go to the beach. I want to try to earn some money.

I'm in tenth grade. I mean, I'm nearly *done* tenth grade. I don't hate school, but I don't love it either. I go to a private school that's not very big. Only about 300 kids go here. Our class sizes are small, so that's good. There are a lot of rules. That's not so good. But they're not too hard to follow, I guess. And we don't wear uniforms. That's good too.

The school is far away from everything. That's bad. We can't go get junk food at lunch. We can't walk anywhere. Some days Dad drives me to school. Other days I have to take the school bus. That's also bad. But it's only on the days Dad works in the city. When he needs to leave really early. Like today. That's about half the time.

I go to a K–12 school. That means we have kids from kindergarten to twelfth grade. Sometimes that's annoying. The little kids can be brats. But they can be cute too.

Right now I can hear them in the music room. It's in a separate building. Probably so the noise won't bother the rest of the school. The little kids are playing drums. Badly! It's funny though.

My friends Sofie and Peter and I are clearing up the kids' playground. We have to make sure everything is put away for summer. The little kids left balls and skipping ropes and Hula-Hoops everywhere. We also find someone's hoodie. And a mitten hidden in a bush. It must have been there since winter.

Now it's an hour until summer break starts. I can't wait. I'm excited to be done with school for a while. I'm also excited because my mom comes home from

Japan tomorrow. She's been there for nearly a month on a business trip. She's a computer programmer.

It's okay just having my dad at home. But I miss my mom. I can't wait to show her my report card. School isn't easy for me, and I worked so hard this year. It paid off. I improved my grades a lot. I think Mom and Dad will be really proud. I'm proud of myself too.

It's just the three of us at home. Me and Mom and Dad. I have a half sister, who has a different mom. But I barely know them. My half sister's name is Mara. She's two years older than me. Seventeen. Dad was married to her mom when he met my mom. It's pretty messy. We don't talk about it much. I know

Dad pays child support for her. And he sees her sometimes. But…yeah. It's messy.

Mara goes to the public high school in Abbotsford. She and her mom live near there. That's not very far from us. We live just over the river in Mission. About a five-minute drive from my school.

Dad calls it a "suburb." But really it's just a small town.

I'd like to get to know Mara better. I've only met her a few times. Once I sent her a message on Instagram, but she never replied. So that was that.

Families can be a lot sometimes.

"Amy!" Sofie calls out to me. "Did you find the other mitten?"

She and Peter walk toward the school. Peter has three Hula-Hoops around his neck. Somewhere, someone's dog starts barking.

"No!" I yell back. "But I found a pair of head-phones!" Another dog barks, like it's mad at me for yelling.

I tug the headphones out of the weeds. Suddenly the ground starts to shake! Sofie and Peter look back at me. Their eyes are wide.

Earthquake!

I expect it to be just a gentle rumble and only last a few seconds. That's happened before. But the rumbling and shaking gets worse. And it doesn't stop. Soon it's like the ground is turning sideways.

Gabrielle Prendergast is an award-winning writer, editor, teacher and designer. She has written many books for young people, including the BC Book Prize–winning *Zero Repeat Forever* and the Westchester Award winner *Audacious*. She is also the author of *Aftershock* in the Orca Anchor line and the Faerie Woods series in the Orca Currents line, which includes *The Crosswood*, *The Wherewood* and *The Overwood*. She lives in Vancouver, British Columbia, with her family.

For more information on all the books

in the Orca Anchor line, please visit

orcabook.com